Little Red Riding Hood

Little Red Riding Hood

Pictures by Karen Schmidt

SCHOLASTIC INC.

New York   Toronto   London   Auckland   Sydney

For my Parents

ISBN 0-590-41881-5

Text copyright © 1986 by Scholastic Books, Inc.
Illustrations copyright © 1986 by Karen Schmidt.
All rights reserved. Published by Scholastic Inc.
Art direction/design by Diana Hrisinko.

21 20 19 18 17 16   5 6/9

Printed in the U.S.A.   23

ONCE UPON A TIME there was a little girl.
Everyone loved her very much.
Her grandmother loved her most of all.
She made her a red velvet hood
to wear. The little girl wore it everywhere.
So she was called Little Red Riding Hood.

One morning, Little Red Riding Hood's mother said, "Your grandmother is not feeling well. Here is a basket of food to share with her. Now hurry along. Remember to stay on the path. And don't stop to play in the woods."

"Yes, Mama," said Little Red Riding Hood. And off she skipped to Grandmother's house.

She had not gone far when she met a wolf. "Good morning, Little Red Riding Hood," said the wolf.

"Good morning, Wolf," said Little Red Riding Hood.

"Where are you going so early this morning?" asked the wolf.

"To see my grandmother," said Little Red Riding Hood.

"And what do you have in your basket?" asked the wolf.

"Good things to eat," said Little Red Riding Hood.

The wolf licked his lips. "The grandmother will be good to eat," he thought. "And this little girl will be even better! I must think of a way to gobble up both of them."

Then the wolf asked, "Where does your grandmother live?"

"Down the path, near the big oak trees," said Little Red Riding Hood. And she pointed the way to her grandmother's house.

Little Red Riding Hood and the wolf walked along the path for awhile. "What a beautiful day," said the wolf. "Why don't you stop to play? Don't you want to pick some pretty flowers?"

Little Red Riding Hood looked around her. "I will pick some flowers for Grandmother," she thought. So she left the path. Each time she picked a flower, she saw a prettier one just ahead. Soon she was deep in the woods.

The wolf ran straight to Grandmother's house.

He knocked on the door. Tap-tap. "Who's there?" Grandmother called.

"It is Little Red Riding Hood," said the wolf in a squeaky voice. "Please open the door."

"I am in bed." said Grandmother. "Lift the latch and come in."

18

The wolf opened the door. He ran into the house. And he swallowed the grandmother in one gulp. Then he put on her nightcap and jumped into bed.

Soon Little Red Riding Hood came to the house. The door was open. "Good morning, Grandmother," she called. There was no answer. Little Red Riding Hood had a strange feeling.

She went up to the bed. There was
Grandmother. But…"Grandmother!"
said Little Red Riding Hood.
"What big EARS you have!"

"All the better to hear you with,
my dear," said the wolf.

"But, Grandmother! What big EYES you have," cried Little Red Riding Hood.

"All the better to see you with, my dear," said the wolf.

"Grandmother!!" gasped Little Red Riding Hood. "What big TEETH you have!"

"All the better to eat you with!" said the wolf.

And he jumped out of bed and gobbled up Little Red Riding Hood. Then the wolf fell fast asleep. Soon he began to snore.

A little while later a hunter walked by. "Listen to the old woman snoring," he said. "I wonder if she is all right."

The hunter went into the house. He saw the wolf fast asleep. "Now I've got you, you wicked wolf," said the hunter. "I have been looking for you for a long, long time." He was about to shoot the wolf. Then he thought that perhaps the wolf had eaten the old woman. She might still be saved.

So the hunter took out his knife. He cut open the wolf.
Out jumped Little Red Riding Hood! "I was afraid in there,"
she said. "How dark it was inside the wolf!"

Then the grandmother crawled out. She was still alive!

Little Red Riding Hood got some heavy stones and put them in the wolf's belly. Then Grandmother quickly sewed the wolf together.

Soon the wolf woke up. When he saw the hunter, the wolf tried to run. But the stones inside him were too heavy. He took one step... two steps... and he fell down dead.

Then Little Red Riding Hood, her grandmother, and the hunter sat down to a fine lunch.

And Little Red Riding Hood thought to herself, "I will never again leave the path to play in the woods. For Mother has told me not to."